First published 2012 by Walker Books Ltd
87 Vauxhall Walk, London SE11 5HJ

This editon published 2013

2 4 6 8 10 9 7 5 3 1

Text © 2012 the Estate of Russell Hoban • Illustrations © 2012 Quentin Blake

The right of Russell Hoban and Quentin Blake to be identified as author and illustrator respectively of this work has been asserted by them in accordance with the Copyright, Designs and Patents Act 1988

This book has been typeset in New Century Schoolbook

Printed in China

British Library Cataloguing in Publication Data:
a catalogue record for this book is available from the British Library

ISBN 978-1-4063-4514-8

www.walker.co.uk

R

MC
2

This Walker book belongs to:

_____

_____

_____

This t

The l
a furth

Russell Hoban & Quentin Blake
Rosie's Magic Horse

WALKER BOOKS

AND SUBSIDIARIES

LONDON • BOSTON • SYDNEY • AUCKLAND

There was an ice-lolly stick with
ice-cold sweetness all around it, white
on the inside, pink on the outside.

Then the sweetness was gone and the stick fell
to the ground. "The sweetness is gone," said the
stick. "No more sweetness."

For a long time nothing happened.
There was wind, there was rain, there
were brown leaves blowing.

Then a hand picked up the ice-lolly stick.

The hand belonged to a girl named Rosie.

She put the stick in her cigar box with the

other ice-lolly sticks.

"Without our ice-lollies we are nothing,"

said the oldest stick.

"I am not nothing," said the new stick.

"I could be something."

"What?" said the old stick.

"Maybe a horse," said the new stick.

"In your dreams," said the old stick.

"We'd like to be a horse, too,"

said some of the other sticks.

That night they dreamed of being a horse.

When Rosie came to say good night to Mum and Dad, they were sitting at the kitchen table shaking their heads over a big pile of bills. "I don't know how we're going to pay these," said Dad.

Before Rosie went to sleep she said, "I wish my cigar box was a chest full of treasure to pay bills with."

She was fooling around with the ice-lolly sticks when she saw that her hands had made an ice-lolly stick horse.

"A horse can't pay the bills," said Rosie, and she fell asleep.

When the clock struck midnight the horse galloped out of the cigar box.

Rosie woke up just in time to jump on its back.

"My name is Stickerino," said the horse. "Where to?"

"Anywhere there's treasure," said Rosie.

"No problem," said Stickerino.

They galloped over cities
and jungles ...

they galloped over oceans and deserts …

until they came to an ice-lolly mountain.

"There it is," said Stickerino. "Ice-cold treasure, sweet and frozen."

"Wrong treasure," said Rosie. "I want the kind that pirates bury in a chest."

"Can do," said Stickerino. They galloped to the other side of the mountain and there was a sandy beach and some pirates with large and small chests full of treasure.

"That's a pretty tough crowd," said Rosie. "How am I going to get some of that gold?"

"Leave it to me," said Stickerino.

He disguised himself as an ice-cream van and jingled his ice-cream tune.

All the pirates came running and queued up for ice-cream while Rosie grabbed the biggest casket she could carry and ran.

One of the pirates saw her. "Stop, thief!" he shouted, and all the pirates started after Rosie.

Quickly Stickerino unvanned himself and became a swarm of flying ice-lolly sticks.

When they hit the pirates they stickled them and kept stickling them until the pirates fell about laughing helplessly.

Stickerino rehorsed himself,
Rosie jumped on his back with her
gold and they were away.

They galloped over deserts and oceans, jungles
and cities until they got home.

The next morning when Rosie's dad came down to breakfast he saw the casket of gold on the table.
"Where's this come from?" he said.

"It's a long gallop,"
said Rosie, and kissed
him good morning.

"It certainly was," said all the sticks.

And they went back to sleep.

Russell Hoban is the renowned author of many acclaimed novels, including *Turtle Diary* and *Riddley Walker*, which won the John W. Campbell Award for science fiction. He also wrote over fifty children's books, including such classics as *The Mouse and His Child*, *Bedtime for Frances*, *The Sea-Thing Child* and, most recently, *Rosie's Magic Horse*. Born in Pennsylvania in 1925, he moved in 1969 to London, where he lived until his death in 2011.

Quentin Blake is one of the world's foremost illustrators, particularly renowned for his collaboration with writers such as Russell Hoban, Michael Rosen, Joan Aiken and Roald Dahl. His books have won numerous awards, including the Whitbread Prize, the Kate Greenaway Medal and the Hans Christian Andersen Award for Illustration. In 1999 he was appointed the first ever Children's Laureate, in 2005 was created a CBE and in 2013 received a knighthood for his services to illustration. He lives in London.

Also by Russell Hoban and Quentin Blake:

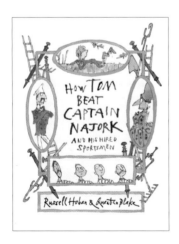

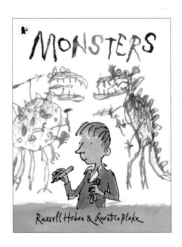

978-1-4063-4383-0   978-1-4063-4382-3

Available from all good booksellers

www.walker.co.uk